Toad
has
Talent

For Mum and Dad

Q Quarto Knows

Inspiring | Educating | Creating | Entertaining

Brimming with creative inspiration, how-to projects, and useful information to enrich your everyday life, Quarto Knows is a favourite destination for those pursuing their interests and passions. Visit our site and dig deeper with our books into your area of interest: Quarto Creates, Quarto Cooks, Quarto Homes, Quarto Lives, Quarto Drives, Quarto Explores, Quarto Gifts, or Quarto Kids.

First published in the UK in 2017 by Lincoln Children's Books
First published in paperback in 2018 by Lincoln Children's Books,
an imprint of The Quarto Group,
The Old Brewery, 6 Blundell Street, London N7 9BH, United Kingdom.
T (0)20 7700 6700 F (0)20 7700 8066 www.QuartoKnows.com

ISBN 978-1-78603-724-4

Illustrated digitally and with watercolour
Set in Bodonitown

Designed by Zoë Tucker • Edited by Katie Cotton and Jenny Broom
Published by Rachel Williams • Production by Jenny Cundill and Kate O'Riordan

Manufactured in Guangdong, China CC072018
1 3 5 7 9 8 6 4 2

Toad
has
Talent

Richard Smythe

Lincoln
Children's Books

On the first full moon
of the winter, when the moon is at
its biggest and roundest, all the forest
animals head to a magical place
called Moonlight Pond.

They go there for a
special reason…

This is where the Moonlight Pond talent
contest is held. The animals rehearse all year
long, ready to perform for the judges.

But last year, there was one little animal
that wanted nothing to do with it...

And that was Toad.

Toad didn't have any amazing skills or tricks.
He couldn't dance, or sing, or do a backflip while knitting
a scarf, and he certainly couldn't blow bubbles as big as his head.

So he hid away in the loneliest, most secret corner of the pond.
"It's best if I keep myself out of sight," thought Toad.
"The others must think I am silly and useless."

The contest finally started.
Toad watched from his lily pad as
The Acrobatic Mouse Troupe
began their performance.

They
wiggled, jiggled,
bounced, and...
jumped!

"I wish *I* could dance as well as the mice,"
sighed Toad, "but my legs and arms
are too long and clumsy."

Next to perform was Snake.
He could bend and twist his body into
funny shapes that made everyone laugh.

He **curled,**
whirled,
looped,
and **hooped**

his way across the ice.

"I wish *I* was funny like Snake," thought Toad, "but I am always grumpy and sad."

After Snake, Duck tried her luck.

Duck and her talented ducklings worked together
and soon had the whole crowd in suspense...

One,

two,

three,

and four!

"I wish *I* could do that,"
thought Toad as he looked on in awe.
"But if I tried, it would all come tumbling down."

Finally, the show came to a close.
But just as the judges were about
to announce the winner,
they heard a shout.

"Wait!"

The call came from a little snail.

"Not everyone has had a go yet.

Toad still needs to perform!"

Everyone turned to look at Toad.
"What about you, Toad?"
asked the judges.

"What's your talent?"

Toad felt very nervous.
He wished more than ever that
he could do something extraordinary!

But just as he stepped out of the
shadows to say that he didn't
have a talent...

He lost his balance
on the ice, and...

slipped
and
tripped,

stumbled
and
fumbled,

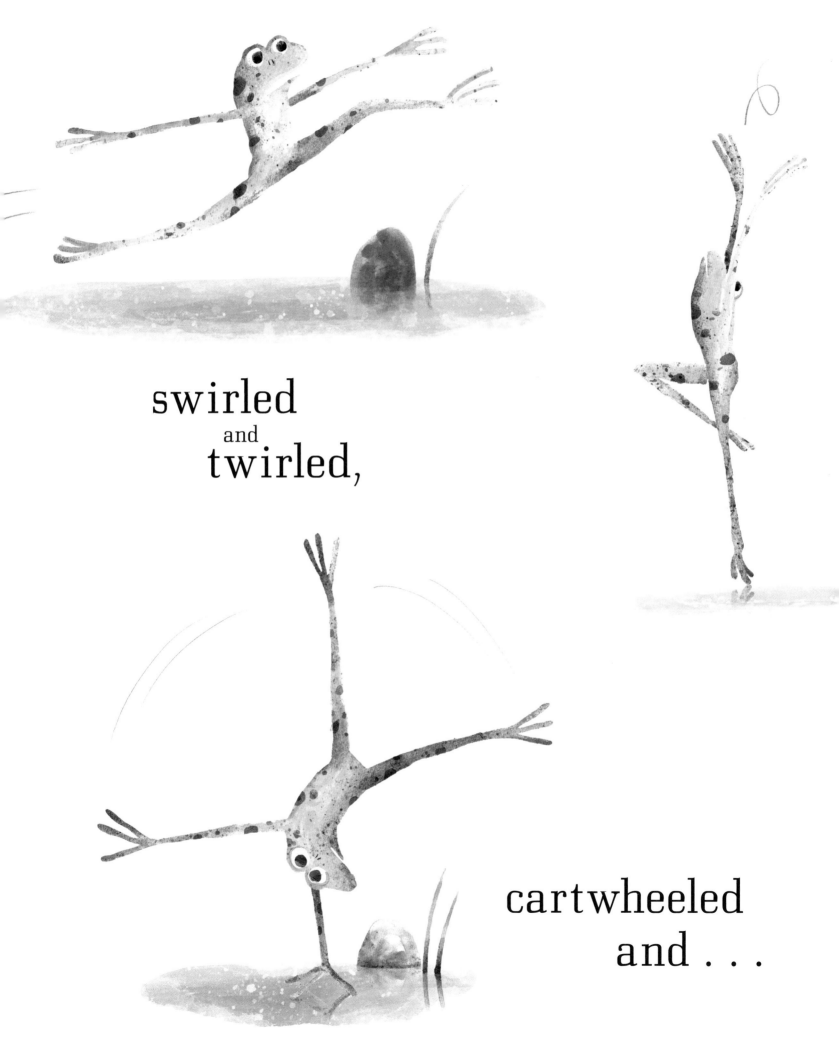

swirled
and
twirled,

cartwheeled
and . . .

slid to a stop at the judges' feet!

Toad lay on the ice, dizzy and embarrassed.
But then he noticed a strange sound...
The other animals were cheering
and clapping for him.

"We've never seen an ice-skating Toad before!" said Bear.

"What unusual and imaginative moves Toad has," commented Owl.

"He's amazing!" shouted Moose.

"Toad
is the winner!"
said all three judges together.

Toad couldn't believe it!

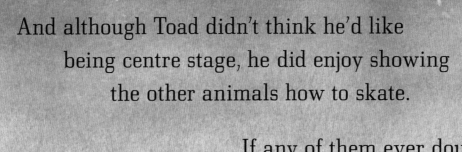

And although Toad didn't think he'd like
being centre stage, he did enjoy showing
the other animals how to skate.

If any of them ever doubted
they could do it, he told them
one important thing...

You never know
what you can do
until you try!

Have you read these other funny stories by Lincoln Children's Books?

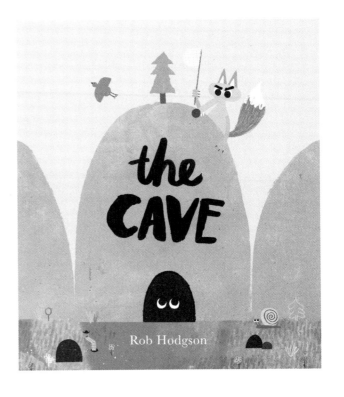

Ralf
Jean Jullien

£6.99

978-1-84780-819-6

Ralf is a little dog who takes up a lot of space.
"Stop getting under our feet!" his family shout.
But one day, Ralf spots smoke coming out of the
house. Could this little dog be the one
to save his family from the flames?

The Cave
Rob Hodgson

£6.99

978-1-78603-116-7

There is a cave. A cave that is home to a creature.
A creature that never leaves its cave…
Because of a wolf. The wolf tries everything to get
the creature to leave the cave, to no avail.
But what will happen when he finally succeeds?

Lincoln
Children's Books